Meg Mackintosh

and

The Mystery at the Medieval Castle

Books by Lucinda Landon

Meg Mackintosh

and

The Mystery at the Medieval Castle

A Solve-It-Yourself Mystery

by Lucinda Landon

Joy Street Books
Little, Brown and Company
Boston   Toronto   London

First edition

Library of Congress Cataloging-in-Publication Data
Landon, Lucinda.
    Meg Mackintosh and the mystery at the medieval castle : a solve-it-yourself mystery / by Lucinda Landon. — 1st ed.
        p.   cm.
    Summary: Meg and her classmates visit a medieval castle and become eyewitnesses to the theft of a priceless silver chalice. The reader is asked to solve the mystery before Meg, using clues found in the text and illustrations.
    ISBN 0-316-51363-6
    [1. Castles — Fiction.   2. Mystery and detective stories.
3. Literary recreations.]   I. Title.
PZ7.L231735Mf   1989
[Fic] — dc19
                                                                88-28586
                                                                    CIP
                                                                    AC

10 9 8 7 6 5 4 3 2 1

BP

Joy Street Books are published by
Little, Brown and Company (Inc.)

*Published simultaneously in Canada
by Little, Brown & Company (Canada) Limited*

Printed in the United States of America

For Jim Egan

Meg Mackintosh peered through her binoculars at the medieval castle. "Look!" she exclaimed. "They're lowering the drawbridge so we can cross the moat!"

"Dundare Castle is the perfect place to relive the Middle Ages," Mrs. Spencer told the history club. "Now don't forget your notebooks!"

As Mrs. Spencer, Nick, Simon, and Liddy started for the drawbridge, Meg quickly checked inside her knapsack. Along with her notebook, she had packed her camera, flashlight, and detective kit — just in case. She swung her knapsack over her shoulder and ran to join the others.

1

"Welcome to Dundare Castle!" A friendly woman greeted them. "I'm Eleanor, Duchess of Dundare, but everyone calls me the duchess. When I was about your age, my family built this castle to look just like our medieval home in Scotland. I've opened it as a museum, and today you're lucky enough to get a private tour."

"Look at her hat!" Liddy whispered to Meg, after Mrs. Spencer had introduced everybody.

"My hat is called a wimple," the duchess explained, overhearing Liddy. "It was worn by ladies in the Middle Ages. My entire staff — Knight Henry, Squire Alfred, Lady Rose, Cook Bernard, and Monk William — all wear authentic medieval costumes. And all of them have experience in the theater, so they know how to speak and act just like people living in the thirteen hundreds.

2

"Now, before I forget, here are some maps of the castle." She passed them out and then marked an **X** on her own. "We're standing here, at the entrance to the courtyard."

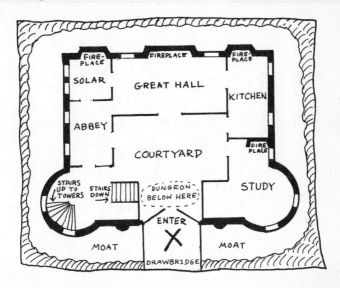

"What's a solar?" asked Nick, examining the map.

"That's my private sitting room," answered the duchess.

"Is that where you keep the chalice that once belonged to a king?"

"A king! It must be worth a fortune!" Simon interrupted.

"I've heard of the chalice," added Liddy. "It's a big silver cup covered with gems."

"It is extremely rare and valuable. It's been in my family for generations," the duchess stated proudly.

"Has anyone ever tried to steal it?" asked Meg.

"Oh, a few times. But it's well protected in the abbey — Knight Henry is on guard."

While the duchess spoke, Meg watched an older man wearing a tunic and tights enter the courtyard and begin replacing the burned-down candles in the candelabra with new ones. After lighting them, he turned to the group and said sharply, "Keep the door shut! The wind keeps blowing me candles out!"

"Fine, Squire Alfred," the duchess replied, as the gruff little man returned to the drawbridge.

4

"He's not very chivalrous," Simon muttered.

"Candles? No electricity?" asked Liddy.

"Not in the thirteen hundreds," Meg replied, loading her instant camera.

Nick walked over to a suit of armor. "Primitive! They even had metal masks for their horses!"

Mrs. Spencer laughed. "The knights were the faithful protectors of the castle. In medieval times, they wore those heavy metal suits in battle. It took three strong men to dress a knight in his armor."

"Say 'cheddar cheese,' Nick!" Meg said as she snapped a photo.

Meg was about to take a second photo when she heard footsteps racing across the stone floor. Suddenly, a dark-cloaked figure dashed out of the shadows and ran across the courtyard. Just before he disappeared into one of the doorways, Meg quickly snapped another shot.

"Who was that?" she asked the duchess.

"That was Monk William. He's been here for many years. He was just running into the abbey — probably late for something as usual."

"Looks pretty suspicious to me," Meg whispered to Liddy. She jotted in her notebook.

"Oh, Meg," Liddy sighed. "You're always looking for a mystery."

Medieval Castle
Time: 10:20
Place: Courtyard
Monk runs into the abbey (little church)
Monk is tall and wearing a dark brown robe, cord belt, and sandals.

A few minutes later, a heavy door creaked open, and Meg turned to see a smiling woman walk gracefully toward them.

"Ah, here is Lady Rose, at last." The duchess introduced them. "Lady Rose will be your guide. She arranges all the tours."

"I'm sorry I couldn't join you earlier, but I had to finish some work in the study," Lady Rose apologized, as she led the group to a glass display case. She pointed to an emblem on one of the rare documents. "This is the wax seal of King Richard, which dates this letter to about eleven ninety."

Gramps would like a picture of that, thought Meg, snapping another photo. It looks like him riding his old horse Charger.

Another door opened, and a stocky, unshaven man wearing an apron came out carrying a tray of food in pewter cups and wooden bowls.

"This is Bernard, the cook in our castle," said the duchess. "He makes a wonderful venison stew." Bernard blushed and nodded hello to everyone.

"Is that tray for Knight Henry?" asked the duchess. "I'll take it to him."

"Thanks, Duchess. I have a joint of beef on the fire to tend to." He headed back to the kitchen.

"Did you see all the blood on his apron?" Meg whispered to Liddy.

"It's from the meat, silly," Liddy said, laughing. As the duchess carried the tray toward the abbey, Lady Rose showed them pictures of shields hanging on the wall. "Each knight wore a coat with his family's own symbolic shield sewn on it. These designs are called coats of arms."

Suddenly, they heard the clattering of dishes, followed by a scream.

"HELP!" cried the duchess from the abbey door. "Knight Henry has been hurt!"

Squire Alfred began yanking on some chains near the entrance. There was a loud CRASH!

"Yikes!" shouted Liddy.

"He's raised the drawbridge!" exclaimed Simon.

"They really put on a good show," said Nick.

"I don't think they're acting," Meg muttered.

"Come on, class, let's find out what happened," said Mrs. Spencer nervously.

They raced to the abbey, meeting Cook Bernard and Squire Alfred at the door.

As she entered the room, Meg smelled burning incense. The cool, damp abbey was dimly lit by candles. The knight lay on the floor.

"Is he all right?" asked Lady Rose.

"He's been hit on the head," answered Cook Bernard, kneeling beside him. "Somebody get water!"

Squire Alfred ran out.

"Oh, poor Henry," cried the duchess.

"He'll be fine." Cook Bernard tried to comfort her. "It looks like just a small knock on the head."

"The silver chalice is gone!" shouted Lady Rose.

The duchess gasped. "Not my family's chalice!"

Meanwhile, Meg had taken out her magnifying glass and was quietly inspecting the scene of the crime for clues.

"Everything must be examined," she told Liddy. "The smallest clue can solve the biggest mystery."

"What are you doing, Meg?" asked Nick.

"Meg is a detective," declared Liddy. "She's going to figure out what happened."

"Sure she is," snickered Nick. "And I'm going to slay a dragon."

Meg busily snapped photos of the room.

"Meg Mackintosh," warned Mrs. Spencer, "it's the police, not the history club, who are going to solve this theft. Duchess, don't you think we should call the police immediately? You do have a telephone, don't you?"

"Yes, of course. There's one in the solar," the duchess replied.

"I'll call them," Squire Alfred offered gruffly, returning with the water. "And don't worry, Duchess, the thief can't escape — I raised the drawbridge."

Just then Nick shouted, "Look!" He reached behind the curtain. "I bet it's the weapon!"

"What is it? Let me see!" Simon urged Nick to give it to him. "It looks like a caveman's club."

"Why, that's the cudgel from the display in the Great Hall!" exclaimed Cook Bernard.

"You're messing up the fingerprints," warned Meg.

"Arrrgh! I challenge thee, Knight Nick!" joked Simon.

Meg rolled her eyes. "They're ruining the evidence," she told Liddy.

"Henry is waking up," said Lady Rose. "What happened?" she asked him. "Do you remember?"

He looked around, confused. "I was just standing here when someone hit me from behind. I fell down." He paused for a moment to think. "The chalice — he took the chalice! I'm sorry, Duchess, I was just too weak to stop him. I remember now! He ran over to the window, opened it, and threw the chalice out! He must have thrown it over the moat to someone waiting on the other side. That's right. I think I heard someone call out to him. And then I think I heard a car race off."

"Wait a minute," Nick interrupted. "I saw somebody come in here right before all this happened. He was acting kind of funny, and I think he had that club in his hand. I bet he did it!"

WHOM DO YOU THINK
NICK SUSPECTS?

"It was the guy in the dark robes," declared Nick.

"Do you mean the monk?" asked Simon.

"I saw the monk!" exclaimed Liddy. She turned and looked at Meg.

"Sure, I saw the monk come in here." Meg nodded slowly. "He did look suspicious." But Meg looked doubtful as she examined her instant photos. Everything just seems too obvious, she thought.

"I think the boy's right," the knight said. "I think it *was* William!"

"Oh, you must be mistaken, Henry!" said the duchess. "Surely William wouldn't have taken the chalice. He's been with my family for ages. I just can't believe he'd do such a thing."

"Where is William?" asked Lady Rose.

"He must have done it," observed Cook Bernard. "Everyone else is here."

"And no one crossed the moat or passed me at the drawbridge," insisted Squire Alfred.

"I'm sorry, Duchess. I like William, too, but I'm quite sure it was him," Knight Henry said firmly. "He *must* be the thief."

"I wish the police would get here," said Mrs. Spencer. "Maybe they could stop the getaway car."

"There was no getaway car," Meg interrupted. "I'm sure the chalice is still in this castle."

WHAT PROOF DOES MEG HAVE?

"Look at these cobwebs in front of the window." She showed everyone with her magnifying glass. "They would have broken if the window had been opened. And all the candles are still lit. It's a windy day. If someone opened the window, the wind would have blown the candles out, just like it did with the squire's candles in the courtyard — or at least it would have blown candle wax on the table. But there's not a drop." Meg turned and looked at the knight. "So it's my guess that the window was never opened, and the chalice is still somewhere in the castle."

There was a long pause.

"Well, wherever the chalice is, Monk William stole it," Knight Henry said finally. "You all saw him run in here."

Meg scribbled on her map, concentrating hard. It did seem as though the monk was the only one who could have done it. Cook Bernard had returned to the kitchen, and Squire Alfred was in the courtyard with everybody else. But no one saw Monk William leave the abbey. So where did he go? And where could he have hidden the chalice?

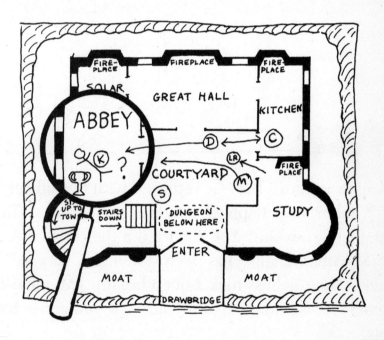

A loud bell rang from across the moat.

"That must be the police," said the squire, running out to lower the drawbridge.

A few minutes later he returned with two officers.

"I'm Sergeant Raphael," said the policeman. "This is Officer Hawkins. You reported a theft?"

"My silver chalice has been stolen. It's very valuable." The duchess took a deep breath. "My guard, Henry, was injured, but he remembers what happened."

"Before you begin your investigation, would it be all right if I took the children back to school?" Mrs. Spencer asked the sergeant.

"I'm sorry, but not yet," he answered. "I'll need a statement from each of you. Officer Hawkins, will you please take the children to another room for a few minutes?"

"Why don't I take them to the kitchen ," suggested Cook Bernard. "We could all use a cup of hot cider."

"Okay," replied the sergeant. "But stay together!"

"Now, class," Mrs. Spencer drew the history club aside. "I want you to forget about this mystery solving. The police will take care of that. Concentrate on writing your reports, and absolutely no wandering about the castle. I'll catch up with you in a few minutes."

"Liddy," Meg whispered, once they left the abbey. "Ask the cook a lot of questions to distract him. That will give me a chance to look around for clues."

"But, Meg, aren't we supposed to let the police handle this?"

"I can't stop in the middle of a mystery! Besides, if I'm right and the chalice is still in the castle, maybe we can find it for the duchess." Meg jotted in her notebook. "And there's something fishy going on here. Why would the knight say that he saw the monk throw the chalice out of the window? If the police listen to him, the wrong person could end up in jail!"

"Okay," Liddy agreed, but she looked a bit bewildered as they entered the kitchen.

While Officer Hawkins checked the kitchen, Cook Bernard poured cider into mugs for everyone.

"Steal from the duchess! I can't believe William would do that!" Bernard walked toward the fireplace.

"Do you do all your cooking over a fire?" Liddy promptly asked him.

"Yes, indeed," Cook Bernard answered, while stirring a pot. "I roast meat on the spit and cook stews in this cauldron. Even when I'm not cooking, I keep the fire lit for warmth. The duchess insists

that all four fireplaces in the castle are always lit. She doesn't like a cold, clammy castle." He tasted some stew from a wooden spoon. "Care for some boiled onions and beans?"

"No, thank you," said Liddy. She glanced at Meg and made a face. "Was the chalice very beautiful?"

"Covered with jewels it was, and worth a pretty penny," answered the cook. "I can see how poor William might have been tempted. The duchess can't afford to pay any of us very much."

"How am I doing?" Liddy asked, when the cook was out of earshot. "Do you think he could have done it? Maybe he slipped through the Great Hall to the abbey without anyone noticing."

"Maybe," said Meg. "He was on his way to the abbey with the knight's tray, but then he let the duchess take it. And there was blood on his apron." She was thinking hard. The staff didn't make very much money, that's a motive for any of them. Whoever stole the chalice could be planning to extract the jewels and sell them one by one. He'd probably get away with it, too.

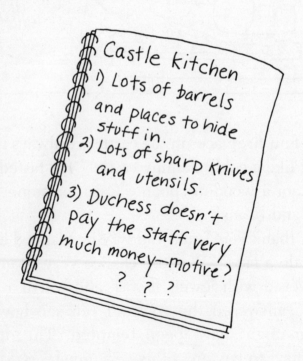

Lady Rose came into the kitchen. She took a tray and placed mugs of cider on it. "The sergeant wants everybody in the Great Hall now," she said as she pushed open the heavy door.

They all followed her into the Great Hall.

"This is definitely an inside job," the sergeant was telling the duchess. "There's no evidence of anyone breaking in. We'd better find this monk. Let's see that map again."

"What about the stairs up to the towers?" asked Officer Hawkins.

"The door there is always locked," answered the duchess. "I have the only key."

"Then I have a hunch the monk headed for the dungeon when he saw that the drawbridge was up. I'll check there first, while Officer Hawkins stays here. Then we'll search the other rooms. How do I get there?" asked the sergeant.

"It's this way," said Lady Rose, pointing to the dungeon stairs on the map.

"Oh, dear," said the duchess. "Lady Rose, how did you hurt your hand?"

"It's nothing," she answered. "I just cut it in the kitchen, a few minutes ago."

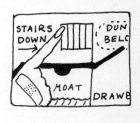

That's strange, Meg thought to herself after Sergeant Raphael had left the room. Why would Lady Rose say that?

WHAT WAS LADY ROSE'S MISTAKE?

Meg shuffled through her photos. *I didn't see Lady Rose cut her hand and besides, she had that bandage on when we first met her,* thought Meg. *I even have a photo of it. What is she trying to cover up?*

Mrs. Spencer peered over her shoulder. "Meg Mackintosh, I hope all those notes are for your report on medieval coats of arms!"

"Not when there's a mystery to be solved!" Meg muttered under her breath, as she tried to cover her notebook.

Just then Sergeant Raphael returned to the Great Hall. With him was Monk William.

"You caught the thief!" shouted Nick.

"I found him sleeping on a cot down in the dungeon," said the sergeant. "He says he's been there all morning."

Monk William looked at the duchess. "I never touched the chalice," he told her. "I was just resting, like I always do," he admitted sheepishly.

"Come on, I want to ask you some more questions at the scene of the crime." Sergeant Raphael and Officer Hawkins led Monk William into the abbey. Everyone else followed them, except Meg and Liddy, who lagged behind.

"Too bad sleeping isn't much of an alibi," Meg whispered, "because this monk is innocent."

"But, Meg, we all saw him run into the abbey."

"We saw a monk, but not this monk," Meg stated.

HOW DOES MEG KNOW?

"The monk we saw was wearing heavy sandals. Remember? We could hear his footsteps coming. The monk with the police was barefoot." Meg showed Liddy her photos and notebook. "And according to my notes, that monk was tall, but this one is short — and the first monk had a cord belt. I think Monk William, the real monk, is being blamed for something he didn't do!"

"Let's go tell the police he's innocent!" sang Liddy.

"Not yet." Meg shook her head. "They'll just say he took off his sandals and belt, and they might not believe my notes. I don't have any hard evidence, so I still can't prove anything."

"If there were two monks, and the real monk was sleeping, then who's the fake monk?" asked Liddy.

"I don't know yet." Meg shrugged. "We need more clues. Let's examine the weapons display."

Cook Bernard was right, thought Meg, as she looked through her magnifying glass. The cudgel must have been taken from this display.

"Those things are ugly — and sharp." Liddy shuddered. "Look! Blood on the floor!"

"Hmmm, that's strange," Meg said quietly.

"What do you mean, Meg?"

WHAT'S SUSPICIOUS ABOUT THE DROPS OF BLOOD?

"How could blood be dripping at the display *before* the knight was hit? There's blood on this sword, too." Meg chewed on the end of her pencil. "The knight lied about seeing the monk throw the chalice out of the window. I wonder if he lied about being hit on the head, too."

"What do we do now?" asked Liddy.

"We still need more evidence to prove that Monk William is innocent. So far, I only know five things for sure.

1) The chalice is still in the castle — WHERE?
2) The knight lied about seeing the chalice thrown out the window — WHY?
3) Lady Rose lied about hurting her hand — WHY?
4) The monk is being framed — by WHO?
5) Drops of blood in the Great Hall before the knight was hit — HOW?

"We'll have to go to the dungeon for more clues," declared Meg. "Are you coming?"

"Oh, all right." Liddy hesitated for a second. Then she and Meg slipped out of the Great Hall.

"This is really creepy," whispered Liddy, as they made their way down the dark stone steps.

"Lucky for us I have my flashlight," said Meg. "We're almost there — I think."

The wooden door creaked as Meg pushed it open. They entered a clammy cell lit by a single torch.

"I don't see the cord belt or the sandals," Meg said, peering under the cot. "That helps prove it wasn't Monk William, but it's still not enough proof. Rats!"

"Please! Don't say that down here!" Liddy cringed and shook cobwebs from her hair.

While Meg studied her notes, Liddy searched the dungeon for clues. "Meg, look at these spots on the wall!"

"It looks like more blood!" exclaimed Meg. She

thought for a moment. "I didn't notice any cut on the monk, and there's no blood on the cot where he was sleeping. Maybe the real thief, the one who stole the cudgel from the display, came down here!"

"This place is getting scary, Meg," said Liddy. "And Mrs. Spencer will be mad. Let's get out of here." She headed for the stairs.

Meg shut her notebook. "Okay, but let's not go up that way."

HOW ARE MEG AND LIDDY GOING TO GET OUT OF THE DUNGEON?

"I have a hunch there's an escape from this dungeon. Look at the stone work, it's different on this wall," Meg said, as she examined the cracks between the stones. "The mortar is loose around this section, and the drops of blood end here. Help me push."

Liddy and Meg leaned hard on the stones, and suddenly one section pivoted to the side and swung open.

"It *is* a secret tunnel!" Meg exclaimed.

"If it's a secret tunnel, then no one would know about it — except the duchess," said Liddy. "Wait a minute! Maybe the duchess took the chalice herself and hid it in here. Maybe she wanted to get a lot of insurance money."

"It is a good motive," Meg admitted, "but the timing of the crime is off. The duchess was with us all morning, and she didn't have much time after she went to the abbey to take the chalice and hide it. It's hard to suspect her." Meg paused for a moment. "But it could have been two people working as a team," she murmured.

She and Liddy started to crawl into the dark, cave-like passage. "If my hunch is right," she told Liddy, "the thief ran down to the dungeon and then escaped through this tunnel. Here, you hold the flashlight while I have a look at the map. This tunnel could lead us to where the real thief hid the chalice."

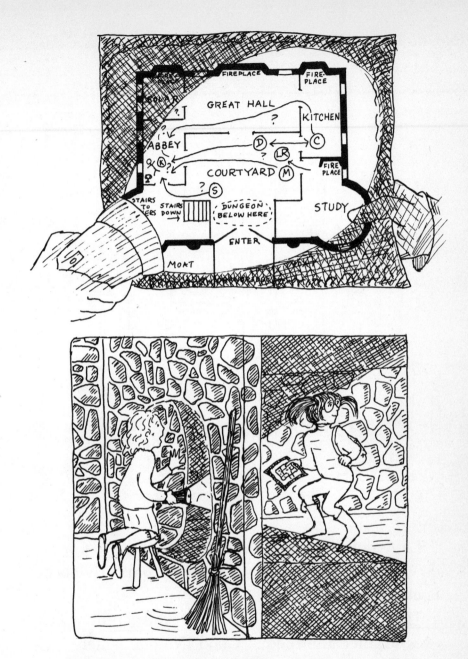

WHERE DO YOU THINK THE TUNNEL GOES?

Liddy followed Meg through the tunnel to a trap-
door. Meg pushed it open to a cool room with lots of
bookshelves.

"This must be the study!" Meg whispered, as her
eyes scanned the room. "Good. No one is here."

"Now what do we do?" asked Liddy.

"We search the room for clues and the chalice."

"But what kind of clues are we looking for?"

"Any evidence that will help prove who the real thief is," said Meg, as she examined the study. "And this room is full of it."

WHAT INCRIMINATING EVIDENCE DOES MEG SEE?

"There are a lot of clues here, Meg." Liddy looked at Meg's photos. "But what does it all mean?"

"A bandage wrapper and a closet full of costumes may not seem like hard evidence," said Meg. "But I think I have enough to prove what really happened."

Just then they heard footsteps coming.

The study door opened and in walked the duchess, followed by Mrs. Spencer, Nick, Simon, Monk William, and Sergeant Raphael.

"Meg Mackintosh! Liddy Robbins! Where have you been! I've been looking all over for you," said Mrs. Spencer. "Sergeant Raphael has been waiting to question everyone together."

Before Meg could respond, Officer Hawkins entered with Lady Rose, Squire Alfred, Cook Bernard, and Knight Henry.

"Why do we have to come in here?" complained Squire Alfred.

"As soon as we have everyone's statement, you'll all be free to go," answered the officer.

"Did you find the chalice yet?" Liddy blurted out.

"Not yet," the sergeant replied. "It seems to have vanished into thin air. We've searched every room on this floor except this one. But we have enough eyewitnesses who say this monk stole it. We're going to take him down to the station."

"I didn't take the chalice. Honest," pleaded Monk William.

"Sure, sure, we know, you already told us," interrupted the officer.

"I certainly don't want to prosecute a dear old friend," said the duchess. "But I do want this settled."

"William, why don't you just confess and get it over with," Squire Alfred urged the monk.

"Maybe the duchess will drop the charges," added Cook Bernard. "She wouldn't want you to go to jail!"

"Wait a minute! Don't confess to anything," said Meg. "Monk William didn't take the chalice."

Everyone turned and stared at Meg.

"Then who did?" asked the duchess.

WHO DO YOU THINK TOOK THE CHALICE?

"We saw a monk, but it wasn't Monk William. It was Lady Rose!" declared Meg. "She was dressed like the monk. See the extra robes in her closet!"

Everyone stared at Lady Rose in disbelief.

"Me? You don't believe this — it's preposterous!" Lady Rose was indignant. "I was with you all morning."

"No, you weren't," said Meg. "You were in the study. You didn't join the tour until after we saw the monk run into the abbey."

"I don't get it." Squire Alfred looked puzzled. "How could Lady Rose run into the abbey dressed as a monk, and then come out of the study?"

"I'll show you," said Meg, getting out her map.

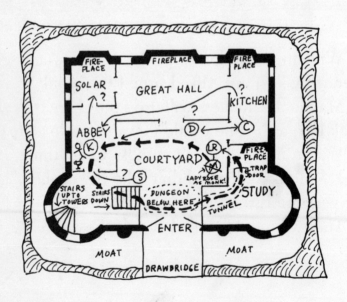

 "Lady Rose dressed up like a monk. Then she took the cudgel, but when she was getting it down from the display, she cut her hand on a sword. She left a trail of blood drops and lied about cutting her hand. That made me suspicious." Meg took a deep breath. "After we all saw her run into the abbey, she stole the chalice and ran down to the dungeon. Then she tiptoed past the sleeping monk and went through the secret tunnel that comes out here in the study." Meg showed them the trapdoor hidden under the rug.

"The old tunnel!" murmured the duchess. "My father put it in for fun. I didn't think anyone but me knew about it."

"What a vivid imagination this little girl has," said Lady Rose. "There is really no proof to any of this. Officers, please. Henry's story is a lot more reliable than this."

"I think we'd better listen to what this young lady has to say," said the sergeant.

"But that's not all," continued Meg. "I think she had a partner, too!"

WHO?

"You!" Meg pointed to Knight Henry. "You and Lady Rose faked the whole scene of the crime! I bet you gave yourself a little bump on the head and then lay down on the floor. You made up the story about the monk throwing the chalice out of the window so we wouldn't search the castle. You should have at least opened and shut the window!"

"You're crazy!" said the knight defiantly. "Who do you think you are, a miniature Sherlock Holmes?"

"Really, this isn't a child's game," Lady Rose pro-

tested. "You all saw the monk run in the abbey, and Henry says that William did it. Isn't that enough proof? And we certainly don't have the chalice!"

"Quick, Meg," Liddy whispered. "Tell them about the bandages!"

"Don't worry, I'll make these thieves give themselves away in two minutes," Meg whispered back.

HOW?

Suddenly Meg started shivering and then sneezed three times. "Gee, I must have caught a chill down in the dungeon. Could we start a fire in the fireplace? It's awfully cold in here," she said.

"Of course, my dear," said the duchess. "This fire is supposed to be going all day." She took a box of matches from her pocket, walked over to the fireplace, and struck a match.

Lady Rose jumped forward.

"Wait! Wait! Don't light it!" she cried. "Don't start a fire. It will ruin it . . . it will ruin the chalice. I hid it in the chimney," she confessed.

The duchess gasped.

"I thought I saw something sparkling up there," Meg explained. "And Cook Bernard said that all the fires were supposed to be going all day."

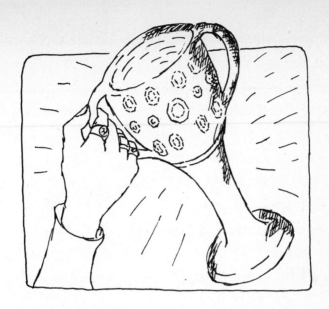

The duchess reached up inside the fireplace. Sure enough, there was the chalice. It had a bit of soot on it, but the jewels were still in place.

"Rose and Henry, how could you?" The duchess was shocked. "How could you steal the chalice and then blame poor William!"

"We figured you wouldn't let William be arrested." Knight Henry tried to explain. "Without the chalice as evidence, we thought you'd drop the charges."

"We wanted to sell the jewels so we could move away and get started in real acting careers," continued Lady Rose. "We had the perfect plan, the perfect eyewitnesses!"

"But you didn't plan on Meg Mackintosh being in the class!" said Liddy proudly.

"Those sneezes were a pretty good performance, Meg," said Nick. "Maybe *you* should enroll in acting school!"

"Brilliant detecting!" Sergeant Raphael congratulated Meg, as Officer Hawkins handcuffed the two thieves and led them away.

"We all thank you very much, Miss Mackintosh," said the duchess warmly.

"Especially me," grinned Monk William, shaking Meg's hand.

Meg blushed a little. "You're welcome," she said.

As the history club started to leave, the duchess went over to a wall display and took down a picture.

"In appreciation of your finding my chalice, I would be honored if you would take this," said the duchess, handing the picture to Meg.

"Wow! It's the coat of arms of the Mackintosh Clan! Thanks, Duchess!" Meg exclaimed. "My Grandfather Mackintosh will love seeing this!" She swung her detective knapsack over her shoulder and ran across the drawbridge.

Another case solved!

HANGING THE COAT OF ARMS

PETER, ME, SKIP, AND GRAMPS

52